THE BRAVE LITTLE PUMPKIN

BY: MANDY FENDER

THIS BOOK BELONGS TO:

WHEN I AM AFRAID, I PUT MY TRUST IN YOU.

PSALM 56:3 (NIV)

HI, MY NAME IS LITTLE PUMPKIN AND, SOMETIMES, I GET SCARED.

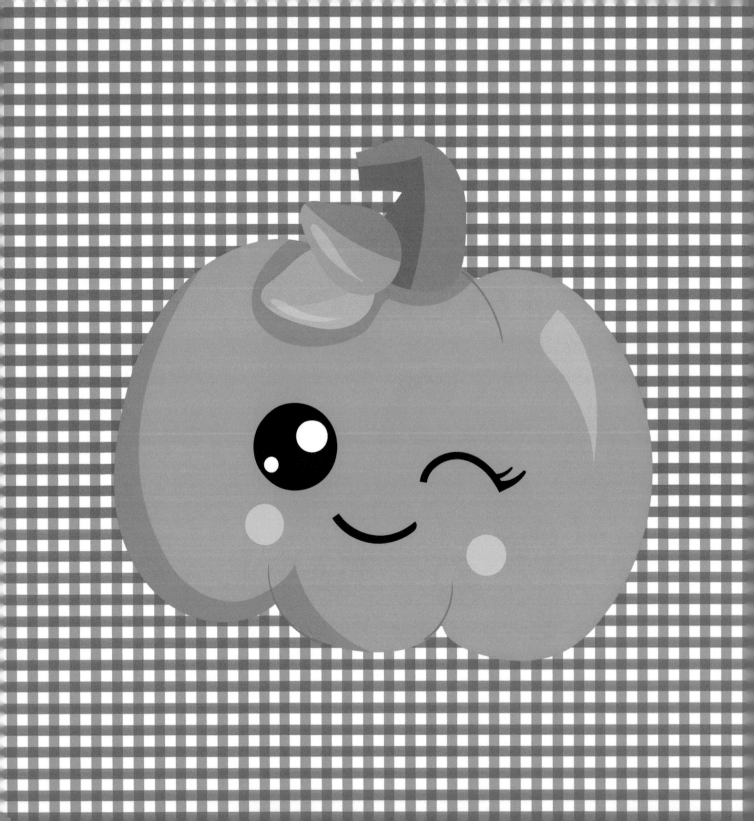

BUT THIS ISN'T A STORY ABOUT ME BEING AFRAID. THIS IS THE STORY OF HOW I BECAME BRAVE!

IT ALL BEGAN WITH MY FRIEND, STAN.

AND IT STARTED WITH A...
SQUEAK!

THEN AN...

I HID BEHIND A TREE BECAUSE I DID NOT KNOW WHAT IT COULD BE.

THEN STAN SAID,
"IT'S JUST ME!"

BUT I WASN'T SO SURE, SO I CLOSED MY EYES TIGHT.

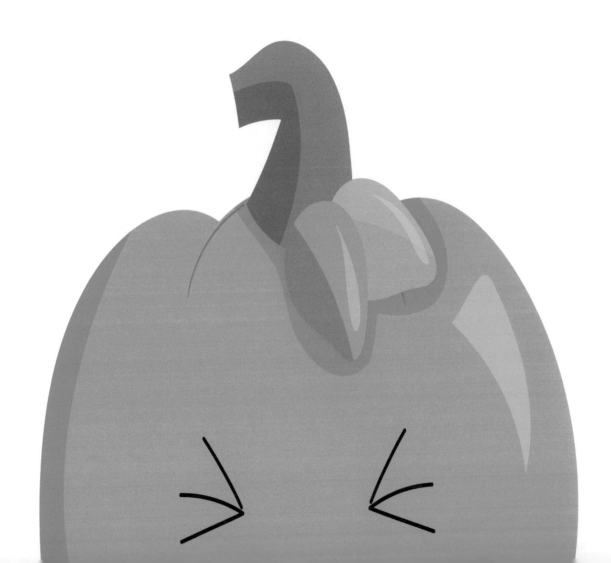

THEN, I REMEMBERED A PRAYER I COULD PRAY AND PRAYED WITH ALL MY MIGHT!

"LORD, WHEN I AM AFRAID,
I PUT MY TRUST IN YOU,
HELP ME BE BRAVE!"

WHEN I OPENED MY EYES, I WASN'T SO SCARED. IN FACT, I WASN'T AFRAID AT ALL.

I FELT BRAVE!

WITH MY EYES OPEN, NOW I COULD SEE, IT WAS JUST MY FRIEND WHO SQUEAKED.

"HI, STAN!"

"HI, LITTLE PUMPKIN!"

"I AM SORRY I SCARED YOU! I DID NOT MEAN TO."

"IT'S OK! IT TAUGHT ME TO BE BRAVE."

THIS IS THE WAY, I LEARNED TO PRAY AND KNEW IT WAS OKAY TO NOT BE AFRAID OF EVERY LITTLE THING!

THE

END

PRAYER

LORD, I THANK YOU FOR ALWAYS BEING WITH ME! WHEN I AM AFRAID, HELP ME REMEMBER TO TRUST YOU! I KNOW YOUR PERFECT LOVE TAKES AWAY ALL FEAR! HELP ME BE BRAVE!

IN JESUS' NAME, AMEN!

THANK YOU SO MUCH FOR
TAKING THE TIME TO READ
THE BRAVE LITTLE PUMPKIN
TO YOUR LITTLE ONE! I PRAY IT
WAS A BLESSING AND HELPED
THEM LEARN TO BE BRAVE,
KNOWING THEY CAN TRUST IN
JESUS!

BLESSINGS,
MANDY FENDER

FROM AFRAID TO BRAVE!

ISBN 9798351557083

9 798351 557083

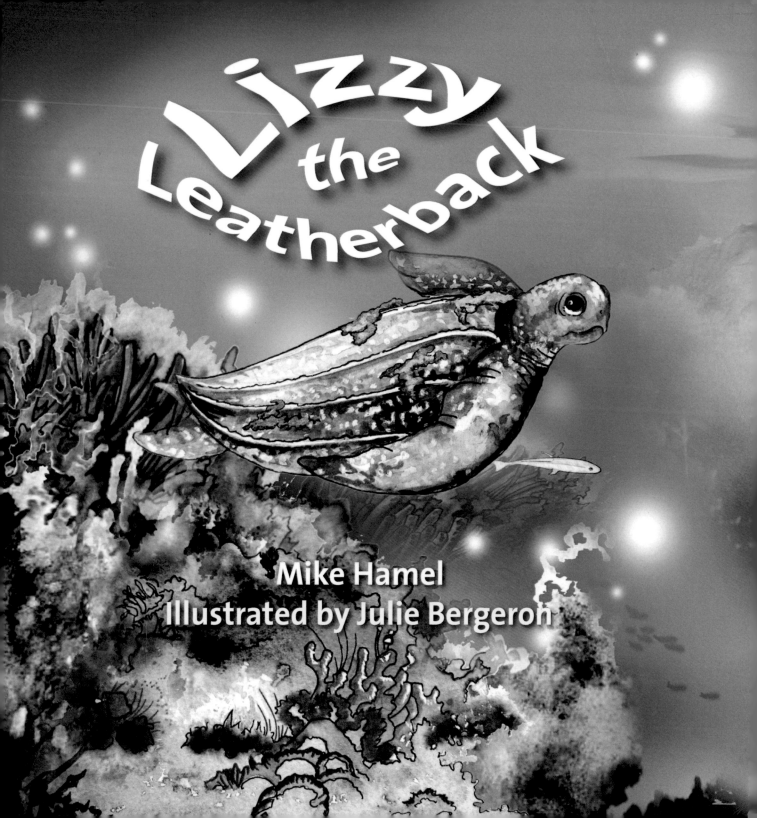

Lizzy the Leatherback

Mike Hamel

Illustrated by Julie Bergeron